Copyright © 2014 by NordSüd Verlag AG, CH-8005 Zürich, Switzerland.
First published in Switzerland under the title *Heule Eule - Nein, ich lasse niemand rein!*
English translation copyright © 2014 by NorthSouth Books Inc., New York 10016.
English translation by Erica Stenfalt. Designed by Pamela Darcy.

First published in the United States, Great Britain, Canada, Australia, and New Zealand
in 2015 by NorthSouth Book, Inc., an imprint of NordSüd Verlag AG, CH-8005 Zürich,
Switzerland.

Distributed in the United States by NorthSouth Books, Inc., New York 10016.
Library of Congress Cataloging-in-Publication Data is available.
Printed in Germany by Grafisches Centrum Cuno GmbH & Co. KG,
Calbe, April 2014

ISBN: 978-0-7358-4129-1 (trade)

1 3 5 7 9 • 10 8 6 4 2

www.northsouth.com

Owl Howls Again!

Paul Friester ✦ Philippe Goossens

North
South

One evening Mommy Owl said, "Little Owl, I'm going out to get your favorite food. Be good and don't let anyone in. Do you promise?"

Little Owl nodded and said, "Yes, Mommy, I'm a big owl now!"

Mommy Owl flew off, and Little Owl locked
the door to their den. **CREAK-CLUNK!**

Little Owl opened her book of fairy tales and found her favorite story, "The Three Little Pigs." She loved looking at the pictures . . .

Suddenly, there was a loud knock on the door.
KNOCK! KNOCK!
Little Owl hopped with fright and cheeped,
"Who's there?"
A voice said, "Let me in, Little Owl. It's me!"

"No!" cheeped Little Owl. "Mommy told me not to let anyone in."

"But I *am* your mommy," called the voice. "I've brought our supper!"

"Anyone could say that," replied Little Owl. "Maybe you're the big bad wolf and want to gobble me up. No, I won't let anyone in!"

So Mommy Owl stood at the door with her bag of
grubs. She didn't know what to do.
Just then, the squirrel was passing and chattered,
"Good evening, Mrs. Owl. Have you just arrived home?"

"Yes," said Mommy Owl.
"But Little Owl won't let me in."

"Oh, we can sort this out," said the squirrel.
She knocked on the door . . . **KNOCK!**
KNOCK! . . . and called, "Open the door,
Little Owl. Your mommy is standing right here.
I can see her clearly!"

"But *I* can't see her!" replied Little Owl. She felt confused and started to cry. "No, I won't let anyone in!"

"That's great!" said Mommy Owl angrily. "Now she's howling as well!"

"Tut, tut! I only wanted to help," huffed the squirrel.

And from the den came the sound of Little Owl: **HOO . . . HOO . . . HOO!**

Next the stag beetle scuttled along and snapped, "What's all this noise?"

Mommy Owl and the squirrel explained, and Little Owl howled.

The stag beetle knocked on the door and called, "Now, enough of this nonsense! I'm standing here with your mother and the squirrel. Open this door immediately!"

But then Little Owl howled even louder. "What? There are three of you, and I am all by myself. No, I won't let anyone in!"

Next, the crow arrived and cawed in amazement. **"CAW!**
What's going on here?"

Mommy Owl and the squirrel explained, the stag beetle
scolded, Little Owl howled, and the crow covered his ears
and did some thinking.

Then he said, "Little Owl is only keeping her promise.
Mrs. Owl must prove to her that she really is her mother."

"But how?" asked Mommy Owl desperately. "After all, she can't see me!"

"Then you need to tell Little Owl something only the two of you would know," explained the wise crow.

Mommy Owl thought for a while. Then she placed her beak against the keyhole.

"Little Owl, I really am your mommy. The big bad wolf wouldn't know our secrets. But I know where you like to be tickled and the name of your favorite fairy tale . . . ." And she whispered their secrets into the keyhole.

Then Little Owl sniffed and asked, "And what is my favorite food?"

"Something I just happen to have here in my bag," said Mommy Owl.

The door of the den opened.
CREAK-CLUNK! And Little Owl
slipped under her mommy's wings and
cheeped, "Can I have ketchup and chips
with it?"